CROWN OF THE COWIBBEAN

written and illustrated by

MIKE LITWIN

ALBERT WHITMAN & COMPANY
CHICAGO, ILLINOIS

for Dad

Library of Congress Cataloging-in-Publication data is on file with the publisher.

Text and illustrations copyright © 2014 Mike Litwin
Published in 2014 by Albert Whitman & Company
ISBN 978-0-8075-8719-5
Printed in China.
10 9 8 7 6 5 4 3 2 1 BP 18 17 16 15 14

For more information about Albert Whitman & Company,
visit our web site at www.albertwhitman.com.

CONTENTS

THE LEAKY Tiki

Everything seemed peaceful and perfect as usual on the tropical paradise island of Bermooda. But from the east, a bold ocean breeze rushed through the palm trees with a rumble that sounded almost like thunder. It was the type of wind that made a cow's fur stand on end, as if the breeze itself knew that something exciting was about to happen.

At the exact same time that breeze bellowed, nine-year-old calf Chuck Porter and his adopted brother Dakota were trotting toward the beach. Mama and Papa Porter said the

1

two of them could camp out on the beach for the weekend as long as they were careful and stayed out of trouble.

"Let's look for a place to put up our tent," Chuck said. He pulled a copy of *The Daily Moos*, the island's newspaper, from his camping pack. "The moospaper said the Silver Cow always shows up at sunset."

That morning, Chuck had read an article in *The Daily Moos* about a mysterious silver cow that appeared in the waves...and then vanished without a trace. The moospaper said it was a mirage, but Chuck took it as a sure sign that the beach was haunted. Chuck loved adventure and he insisted they had to investigate right away.

This was nothing new, of course. Chuck was always on some kind of mission. That's how he met Dakota. Dakota was not a calf at all, but a hu'man boy in a cow costume. A few months ago, Chuck was exploring a forbidden shipwreck and found Dakota—a lost hu'man boy washed up on a sandbar with no home, no family, and no idea where he was. They became best friends, even though the island legend said hu'mans were extinct, savage monsters. Chuck disguised his new friend's identity with "cowmouflage"—a cow costume made from coconut shells, a sea sponge, and an old blanket. The Porters adopted Dakota when they learned that he had no family, but they still had no idea that he was a hu'man. No hu'man had *ever* been on Bermooda before, so Chuck and Dakota decided to keep it a secret.

The two of them had just found an excellent campsite when Dakota noticed something in the distance.

"What's that?" he said, pointing to a ship

at the end of the harbor. "I haven't seen that ship before."

Chuck looked up and gasped. "The *Swashclucker*!" He started off toward the village, still wearing his camping pack. "Come on! We can go listen to Marco Pollo!"

"Who's 'Marky Po-yo'? What about building our tent?" Dakota asked. But Chuck was already charging up the beach and didn't answer. Dakota rushed to catch up.

They clomped all the way through the village to the edge of the harbor, with Chuck's little white cow tail swishing excitedly the whole time. They finally stopped at a small, rickety-looking tavern with bamboo walls and a straw roof. Outside stood a wooden post with a grinning cow's face carved into it. An orange bandana with white polka dots was tied around its head, and water trickled out

from between its enormous teeth. Above the post was a sign that read "The Leaky Tiki."

"So who's Marky Po-yo?" Dakota repeated as he caught his breath.

"It's not 'Marky'. It's *Marco*," Chuck corrected him. "Marco Pollo is the most daring explorer to sail the sea!" he explained, waving his hooves. "The *Swashclucker* is his ship. Lots of folks have sailed around Bermooda, but no one has sailed as far away as Marco. He's been to the horizon and beyond! He's amazing!"

Chuck opened the squeaky old door to the Leaky Tiki, and they entered a big, warmly lit room filled with tables and chairs. In the middle of the room, a circle of cows gathered around a pint-sized rooster who was perched on a table and chattering wildly.

This is Marco? Dakota thought as they inched to the front of the crowd. Marco was quite small for someone with such a big reputation. He stood no more than two feet high. His deep maroon captain's hat was almost as big as he was, with ruffled white trim and a huge yellow plume. He fluttered his feathery wings and squawked excitedly.

Marco always roosted at the Tiki when he came in from a voyage, filling the tiny pub with colossal tales of adventure starring him and his first mate Ribeye. Even though his stories were very entertaining, almost no one took them seriously. After all, nearly everyone who lived on the island believed Bermooda was the only life in the sea. Everyone but Chuck, of course.

Chuck couldn't get enough of Marco's stories. Whenever he saw the *Swashclucker* docked in the harbor, he would scurry to the Tiki and listen to Marco cackle on for hours about sea monsters, treasures, and far-off lands. It was the kind of life Chuck could only dream of living. Marco was his hero.

"So there we were," Marco clucked, "both of us wrapped up tight in the giant squid's tentacles. Of course, Ribeye here was helpless to fight." He motioned behind him to an enormous bull with an eye patch. Ribeye stood with his arms crossed, quietly frowning and shaking his big square head.

The chicken continued, "I alone, *Marco*, with my cunning, my prowess, my—"

"Bull-oney!" mooed a large cow from the back of the crowd. The whole circle of cows laughed. "Pollo, every time you tell that story, that squid gets bigger and bigger."

The laughter grew louder as Marco turned red beneath his orange feathers. But the cows' laughter did not stop Marco. He continued to talk…and talk…and talk. Every once in a while, Ribeye would just shake his head and grunt while rolling his one good eye.

Chuck and Dakota listened for nearly two hours before remembering they were supposed to be camping. They quietly slipped out of the Tiki as Marco was telling the crowd about the time he cut off the head of a giant sea snake.

"See? I told you Marco was amazing," Chuck said.

"Are you kidding?" Dakota answered, raising an eyebrow. "It all sounds like a bunch of fairy tales to me." Dakota was not as quick to believe Marco's epic stories as Chuck was. He thought it was ridiculous enough that they were spending their weekend looking for a silver ghost cow in the ocean, let alone stories about sea snakes and giant squids.

"They're not fairy tales!" Chuck snapped back. "Marco is a great explorer and a hero! It's the truth!"

"No, *this* is the truth," Dakota held up their copy of *The Daily Moos*. "This is stuff that really happened."

Chuck sighed. As a hu'man, Dakota knew just as well as him that there really was a whole other world out there. *Shouldn't he believe Marco more than anyone?* Chuck thought to himself. He glanced at the *Swashclucker*.

Chuck's tail began to twitch. "I've got an idea!" he said. "I can prove Marco's stories are true."

"How?" Dakota asked nervously. Whenever Chuck had a great idea, it usually ended up getting both of them in trouble.

Chuck pointed to the *Swashclucker*. "Let's go on a treasure hunt."

"A treasure hunt?" Dakota echoed. "We're already on a ghost hunt! What about our camping trip?" Dakota was not as daring as Chuck, and he preferred camping on the beach much more than poking around a ship they didn't own.

"We still have plenty of time before sunset," Chuck assured him as he strolled toward the harbor. "Come on, it'll be an adventure."

I hate adventure, Dakota thought.

‖

2
TREASURE TROVE

The *Swashclucker* was docked at the very end of the wharf. Marco loved attention, so he always docked where everyone could see his boat. Sneaking on board was going to need a careful plan. Luckily, Chuck was always full of plans.

"Put this on," he said as he handed Dakota an orange bandana with white polka dots. "It's your disguise."

"A disguise on top of my cow disguise? This is silly." Dakota took the bandana from Chuck. "This looks familiar. Isn't this the bandana from the post outside the Leaky Tiki? Did you steal this?" he gasped.

"It is from the Leaky Tiki, but I just borrowed it. We'll bring it back," Chuck said. "Tie it around your head. All sailors wear bandanas on their heads. Unless you're the captain. Then you wear a hat."

"Is this your plan?" Dakota asked nervously. "What if we get caught?" Marco's first mate Ribeye looked awfully big and mean, and Dakota didn't like the idea of making that one-eyed bull any grumpier.

"We won't get caught," Chuck said as he folded their copy of *The Daily Moos* into a very fine-looking paper hat. "Marco will be busy talking for hours. Besides, we're not going to *take* anything. We're just *looking*. If anyone asks, just say you're one of his sailors."

"Why do *you* get to wear a hat?" he asked Chuck.

"We only have one bandana," Chuck said, putting on the paper hat. "Plus, it's *my* idea, so I get to wear the captain's hat."

They looked out at the wharf. Many cows were milling about, tending to the small boats on either side of the dock.

"There's no way this is going to work!" Dakota said in a hushed whisper.

"Sure it will! Just talk like a sailor," Chuck whispered back. "Arrrr, matey!" he said in a loud pirate voice as he marched out on the pier. "It sure be a good day for sailin', aye?"

"Aye, aye, sir!" Dakota shouted back. "Ummm….Yo ho ho and a bottle of milk!" Dakota's face turned red under his cow mask. He felt incredibly foolish. Cows all over the harbor watched curiously as the two phony sailors marched by, but no one questioned them. Chuck's plan was working! They continued their loud parade all the way to the end of the wharf.

The *Swashclucker* may have been the biggest ship in the harbor, but that was only because all the other boats were so small. Up close the ship was squat and dumpy. Its sides had been repaired so many times that the patchwork of planks nailed to its sides looked like big wooden bandages. At the top of the mast sat a rickety crow's nest with a tiny orange flag waving from it. It really wasn't very fancy. But as far as Chuck was concerned, it was amazing.

"This is such a bad idea," Dakota said as they climbed on board the ship's main deck. "I don't think we're going to find anything here but trouble."

"Weren't you listening to Marco's stories?" Chuck asked. "Even if he's only done *half* the stuff he says, this boat should still have treasures *all over* it! Let's look for that sea snake's head

16

he was talking about! I bet it's in his quarters."

They made their way to Marco's cabin, which looked a lot like a chicken coop. Chuck swung open the door with excitement. He thought the room would be filled with ancient artifacts and mystical objects, glittering jewels and gold coins...maybe the sea snake's head would even be mounted on the wall!

But the cabin was not at all what Chuck expected.

There were no treasures. There were no jewels or prizes or coins. The only golden thing in sight was a warm light that came through the windows, highlighting a globe, a spyglass, and measuring tools on a table in the middle of the room. In the corner was a roosting perch where Marco would stand as he slept. The wall on the right displayed a collection of swords. The wall on the left was covered with maps and charts. It looked like a great place to plan an adventure. But it was no treasure trove.

"Okay," said Dakota. "Where's all the treasure?"

"Of course someone as smart as Marco Pollo wouldn't keep his treasures in the first spot everyone would look. What was I thinking? He hid them in a place that's harder to get to. This boat should have some kind of cargo area, right?" Chuck thought aloud. "A storage place where Marco keeps all his stuff? Let's look in there."

After poking around a bit, Chuck and Dakota found the cargo area in the very bottom of the ship. They climbed down a rope ladder into the room through a hatch in the ship's deck. It was dark and damp, and they could see very little by the dim light that came in from the open hatch. There wasn't much to see, anyway. It was mostly just stacked-up barrels of food and supplies.

Chuck was disappointed and Dakota was not impressed. They both inched a little closer into the darkness, looking for something— *anything*—interesting.

"I don't get it," Chuck said. "I *know* those stories *have* to be true. They just have to be!" He stomped the floor with his hoof. "Some treasure hunt!"

Just then, they heard a long squeak and a loud thud, and the room went from dim to pitch black. Someone had closed the door to the cargo hold.

Chuck scrambled up the rope ladder. "Hey! HEEEEYYYYY!!!" he mooed, banging his hoof on the bottom the hatch. But it was no use. The hatch door was thick and heavy, and no one could hear.

Then the whole room suddenly shook, causing Chuck to fall off the rope ladder. He landed on Dakota with a thud. The floor seemed to move underneath them, rocking back and forth as they tried to stand up on their wobbly legs.

"Are we...*moooving?*" Chuck mooed in a panic.

"I told you this was a bad idea!" Dakota shouted in the dark.

3
ALL ABOARD

Chuck and Dakota searched for a way to get out of the cargo area as the boat rocked back and forth. Dakota tried his best not to be sick as his stomach flip-flopped from all the swaying.

Peering up, Chuck noticed a small crack of light slicing through the dark above their heads. "Look!" he said. "Up there! Light!"

They both climbed onto some barrels to get a closer look. "Come on, give me a boost," Chuck said as he climbed up on Dakota's shoulders. Sure enough, he found a sliver of daylight peeking past a loose board near the ceiling. Chuck pounded his hoof on the board until it broke with a *CRACK!*, creating a hole just big enough to poke his head through. Looking down, he saw waves splashing against the bottom of the boat. Looking up, he saw the side rail of the ship just within reach.

"Hurry! Hurry!" Dakota whined from below. Chuck was rather beefy for such a small cow, and his hooves weighed heavily on Dakota's shoulders. Suddenly, Dakota's knees buckled and gave way. They both tumbled off of the barrels and onto the floor.

"The ship's rail is just above the ceiling," Chuck grunted as he got back to his feet. "But I'm too big to fit through the hole. *You'll* have to do it."

Dakota's face fell. "*Me?* This was all *your* idea, captain!" Dakota was not fond of heights, and the idea of climbing around the outside of a ship on the open water did not thrill him.

"You're smaller and lighter than me," Chuck insisted as he nudged Dakota back up the barrels. "Just grab the rail, climb up, open the hatch, and let me out. Come on, it'll be easy!"

Dakota groaned as he climbed up onto Chuck's shoulders. Chuck always had a way of making his plans sound a lot easier than they actually were. Dakota wriggled himself through the hole Chuck had made in the hull.

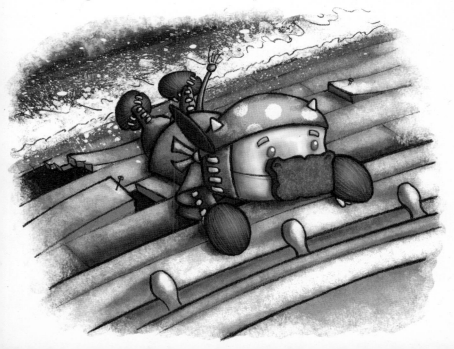

He looked down at the rushing water below, and his stomach churned even more than it had in the rocking cargo area. With a deep breath, he reached up and grabbed the top edge of the ship. But talking about climbing up to the deck was much easier than actually doing it. As he tried to pull himself up, his fingers slipped and he went tumbling down the side. He caught himself on one of the ship's loose boards just before he hit the water. His feet dangled over the waves as he struggled to pull himself up.

"What's going on out there?" Chuck called from inside. "Come on, mooooove it!"

Dakota swallowed a lump in his throat as he began the climb again. He scaled the side of the ship, trying not to look down at the water as he grasped the different boards stuck to the hull. At that moment, he was very thankful that the *Swashclucker* had so many odd pieces of wood nailed to the side of it. Finally, Dakota reached the top. Grunting with effort, he hoisted himself over the ship's rail and plopped onto the main deck. He crawled to the hatch and opened it. Chuck poked his head out of the hatch, quite happy to be free from the dark room.

Squinting his eyes in the daylight, he immediately noticed two things. First, he noticed that they were completely surrounded by water, and Bermooda was nowhere in sight. Second, he noticed that Marco and the very large Ribeye were standing over them.

"*Buon Giorno*, little stowaways," Marco said, his wings on his hips. "May I help you?"

"Oh. Ummm…*lo'hai*," Chuck answered with a wave and a nervous chuckle.

Neither Marco nor Ribeye seemed

very happy to have found them aboard. They brought Chuck and Dakota up to the quarterdeck for Marco's questioning while Ribeye steered the ship.

"Little cows, why are you here?" he asked.

Neither of them wanted to admit that they had been sneaking around his boat looking for treasure. "I guess…we just…wanted to hear more of your stories?" Chuck stammered.

"If you wanted to hear more of Marco's stories, you could have just waited until I came back to port like everyone else," Marco said.

"Can't you just swing back by Bermooda and drop us off?" Dakota asked with a shrug.

But Marco just looked past them at the horizon. "No, little one. I do not think that is possible."

Ribeye grunted and snorted at Marco. Chuck and Dakota had no idea what he was saying, but Marco seemed to understand just fine. They appeared to be arguing.

"I don't want them aboard any more than you do," Marco said in a loud whisper. "But we have the wind on our side! We can't just turn around and take them back to Bermooda!"

Ribeye grunted and snorted some more.

"Yes, I know a ship is no place for little calves," Marco answered. "But we are not turning back! We just find something for them to do, give them a little adventure, we have them back before you know it!"

"Adventure?" Chuck said.

Marco turned his head toward Chuck and Dakota, as though he had forgotten they were standing right there.

"Ribeye, guide us while I greet our new

guests," he said. He led Chuck and Dakota to his cabin.

"My grumpy friend and I ought to drop you stowaways on the first dot of land we see," Marco said, turning to the calves. "But I would never do that to someone who enjoys my stories. Bermooda is already out of sight and I'm afraid it is too late to turn back now. So, until we finish our journey, you shall be my ship's helpers. You are now…buccowneers."

Chuck felt his heart leap inside his chest. "Really? US?"

"BUT FIRST…you must take the oath!" Marco said. He puffed out his chest. "Do you solemnly swear to follow any and all of the captain's orders, to bravely seek adventure, and to not bring bad luck upon the ship and her crew?"

"Aye, aye, captain!" they replied.

"Be warned, my young friends," Marco continued, pointing a feather at them. "This is not a place for cowards, and this is not a playground. This is a daring quest for treasure!"

Chuck's ears perked up. "Treasure?" he repeated. Was he finally on a real treasure hunt?

"*Certamente!*" Marco held up the rolled paper. "This map has been passed down through my family, all the way from my great, great grandfather—Pinfeather Pollo. It will lead us to the greatest treasure in the Cowibbean Sea!"

With a flourish, Marco unrolled the paper. On the paper was an old map featuring tropical islands, a coral reef, a shipwreck, and a rock with a red "X" scratched over it. A sailing path was drawn out in a dotted line that looped and curled around the landmarks, making a giant "S".

"First, we-a start here, at *Cattleena*," he pointed to a little island with a palm tree in the lower left corner of the map. "Then we sail northeast, to *Waterdown*—the treacherous yard of underwater shipwrecks!"

Dakota's neck hair rose at the mention of shipwrecks. It reminded him of the *H.M.S. Hortica*—the forbidden Bermooda shipwreck where he had been found.

Marco hopped up on the table, clucking louder and louder. "Then we swoop around to Sterling Reef," he went on feverishly, "home of the most magical maids of the sea!" He got so excited that he drew his sword from its sheath.

"Then…it's on to Spidercrab Rock!" he shouted, fluttering to the top of his globe. "Where we shall find the greatest treasure known! *The Coral Crown*!" Brandishing his sword high in the air, he threw back his head and ended his speech with a long crow.

"The Coral Crown?" Chuck asked. He loved legends and stories, but this was one he had not heard before.

"The Coral Crown is the most beautiful, most exquisite prize in all the Cowibbean." Marco explained, waving his wings slowly. "It is said to be made of gold coral from the deepest parts of the ocean. It is covered in emeralds and sapphires…and diamonds as big as your eye! A trophy worthy of the highest king!"

"Wow!" Chuck said, his eyes growing wide. "Has anyone ever seen it?"

"Ahhh…no." Marco lowered his head. He suddenly looked sad. "Many roosters of my family have looked for the crown. My grandfather has told me the tales since I was a little chick. Legend say the crown rests at Spidercrab Rock. He spent his *whole life* searching for it. He followed this map many times. But no matter how far he sailed…he never found the crown. No one has."

Of course no one's ever found it, Dakota thought to himself. *It probably doesn't even exist.* Just as before, he was not so impressed with Marco's tales.

"What's this?" Chuck asked, pointing to a

poem scribbled at the bottom of the map. He read the verses aloud:

"Circle of darkness, horn of the heavens,
A watery grave where the clock strikes eleven,

A spying eye sees when our own eyes do fail,
Into the nothingness, bravely we sail.

The beast shall sleep at the Sea-Cows' song,
And we shall be guided by stars of our own.

Reach for the skies and a sea rover finds
The crown she doth sing to a key of her kind.

And guard thy heart, hearties, where wishes
    do dwell,
For those who bring ruin shall earn it as well."

"Huh?" Dakota wrinkled his nose under his cow mask. "I don't understand any of that."

"There's nothing to understand," Marco said. "It's just a shanty. An old sea tune my grandfather sang for good luck."

"It almost sounds like a bunch of clues," Chuck said.

"Poppycock!" Marco snapped. Who needs clues when we have a map? This map will help Marco succeed where all others have failed. Everyone who has looked for the crown has given up, gotten lost, or perished at sea."

"Maybe if they'd just gone straight to Spidercrab Rock, they wouldn't have had so much trouble," Dakota suggested. He pointed at the map. "See? First you go all the way east to some old shipwreck. Then you sail all the way west to this coral reef. Then you come back east again to Spidercrab Rock!" He drew an invisible line through the middle of the path with his coconut shell hoof. "Wouldn't it be easier to just go in a straight line?"

Marco lowered his eyelids and stared at Dakota as though he were crazy. "If it were that easy, little cow, don't you think someone would have done it by now?"

"Maybe it's another clue," Chuck offered. "There must be some reason to take that big curvy path."

"There are no clues!" Marco clucked impatiently. He was beginning to tire of these stowaway calves telling the great Marco Pollo how to read a map. "That poem is just a silly old song, and we sail that path because THAT IS WHAT'S ON THE MAP."

At that moment, they heard Ribeye grunt loudly from the quarterdeck above.

"What was that?" Dakota asked.

"Ribeye says '*Land Ho!*'" Marco answered, rolling up the map and stuffing it under his gigantic captain's hat. They all joined Ribeye up at the ship's wheel. The sun was beginning to set now, and it reflected in the ocean like tiny droplets of fire. In front of the beautiful sunset was a tiny little island.

Marco gazed ahead at the island through his spyglass. "Behold…Cattleena!" he said.

Cattleena was much smaller than Bermooda. There weren't as many palm trees, and the sand looked a lot rockier. The cluster of wooden docks lining the side of the island looked old enough to fall apart. It wasn't much, but it still looked pretty enough in the pink rays of the setting sun.

Dakota furrowed his brow as he remembered their abandoned ghost hunt. "So much for finding the Silver Cow at sunset," he muttered. He pulled the paper hat off of Chuck's head. "We were *supposed* to spend the weekend *camping*! What's Mama going to say?"

Chuck couldn't understand what Dakota was so cranky about. After all, Mama wouldn't expect them home from camping for a couple of days. For now, the breeze was warm, the sunset was lovely, and they were searching for a priceless treasure with a genuine hero. What could possibly go wrong?

4

THE BLACK SPOT

Marco shouted orders to his crew as they docked the *Swashclucker*. "So what are we doing here?" Dakota asked.

"Cattleena is where the map starts, so that's where we start," Marco stated firmly. "We dock here for the night before beginning our voyage."

Even though Marco said the poem didn't have any clues in it, Chuck was convinced that it did. He was even more convinced he would find the answers to some of those clues here on Cattleena.

"Can we walk into town?" Chuck asked. "I promise we'll be careful."

Ribeye snorted his disapproval, but Marco dismissed it.

"Oh, let them go, Ribeye. Let them have a little fun!" he clucked. "Just don't tell anyone about our voyage," he warned them. "And stay away from The Black Spot. That place is nothing but trouble. And *definitely* stay away from the Kingfish."

"Who's the Kingfish?" Chuck asked.

"The Kingfish is a dirty scoundrel," Marco said. "He runs most of this place, and he is not too fond of cows. He takes whatever he wants, whenever he wants, and he'd love to find the crown as much as we would."

"He sounds like a pirate," Chuck noted.

"*Sí*," Marco agreed. "A pirate of the worst kind."

39

"Sounds like a regular bully to me," Dakota mumbled.

Chuck and Dakota found that Cattleena was not as pretty up close. Everywhere they looked, the town was dirty and rough. Even worse, Chuck hadn't found any answers to clues. He was about to suggest they go back to the *Swashclucker* when he saw something he couldn't resist. The tavern just ahead of them had a dirty white sign with a dark black circle on it. Written inside the circle were the words, "The Black Spot."

"Look!" Chuck said, drawing a circle around the black circle with his hoof. "A 'circle of darkness!' Just like in the poem!"

"Couldn't it just be a coincidence?" Dakota asked.

Chuck reached for the door. Dakota slapped his hand over it. "No! Marco said to stay away from here! Besides, the last time we went into a place like this, it was the Leaky Tiki…and look how much trouble that brought us!"

Chuck pushed Dakota's hand aside. "Come on," he said, opening the door. "How bad could it be?"

The Black Spot looked nothing like the Leaky Tiki. This place was not warm and cozy. This place was gloomy and cold. The room was dimly lit by ship's lanterns hanging from the ceiling. The air tasted salty and stale, and

the whole place smelled of fish. The windows were covered with brown palmetto leaves that had dried up long ago. A sad-looking octopus served drinks with as many hands as he could spare to a rowdy band of lobsters, crabs, and other shellfish. They laughed loudly as they played cards and slurped plankton at their tables. This place really was a circle of darkness. Chuck and Dakota pulled up two bamboo stools at the counter.

"What are we looking for?" Dakota asked.

"Well, the poem says '*Circle of darkness, horn of the heavens*'," Chuck said. They looked at their dingy surroundings. There was nothing heavenly about this place. "There has to be something here," Chuck insisted. "I just know it."

Dakota sighed. "Maybe there is no 'Horn of the Heavens'. Maybe there is no Coral Crown. I know you want to believe that Marco is a great explorer. But maybe he's just a great storyteller."

Chuck pretended not to hear. "You know what's weird?" he whispered. "This island is called 'Cattleena' but I haven't seen any cattle."

"I know," Dakota agreed. "Other than you, the only cow in this place is that statue over there." He pointed to a small cow statue on a round black pedestal in a dark corner of the room. They tiptoed over to take a closer look.

The statue was made of white marble. It was shaped like a cow with angelic wings and an elegant crown. A single horn stuck out from the center of the cow's head. Squinting his eyes, Chuck read the words engraved on the statue's base: "Nalani, Heifer of the Heavens."

"What is it?" Dakota asked. "A unicow? There's only one horn."

"This must be it!" Chuck said. "The 'Horn

43

of the Heavens'!" He peered closer and noticed a very small latch on the back the of the horn. "I think this thing comes off," he said. He wiggled on the horn.

"Careful! You'll break it!" Dakota said in a hushed voice.

Chuck tugged a little harder, and the horn came off with a gentle *click!*

The two glanced around nervously but no one in the place seemed to notice them. Chuck and Dakota looked closely at the horn and now saw that it was hollow on the inside. Six tiny holes had been bored through the side.

"Hey! It's not just a horn!" Chuck said. "It's a horn*pipe!*"

Chuck turned the hornpipe flute over, and a roll of yellowed paper fell out from inside. They unrolled the paper to find an odd scale of musical notes that twisted and wound all over the page in the shape of a crown. Below the musical notes was a list of what seemed to be song titles, scribbled in a familiar handwriting:

The Fishes' Breath
Song o' the Sea-Cow
Tempest and the Tide
Fire in the Heavens

"Look! It's the same handwriting as Marco's map!" Chuck's hooves quivered with excitement. "Now do you think it's all just a coincidence?"

"It still doesn't make sense," Dakota insisted. "We're on Cattleena, there's a cow statue… where are all the cows?"

"The Kingfish hates cows," said a raspy voice behind them. They turned to see a big black parrot perched at the end of the counter. "Forgive me," the old bird croaked, "I couldn't help but overhear. The name's Nwar. And the answer to your question is that the Kingfish has hated cows, hated cows ever since one of them cut off half his whiskers."

Nwar looked like a tough old bird, but very tired. His heavy black feathers were tattered and his eyes had saggy red rims. He seemed awfully happy to have someone to talk to, so Chuck and Dakota listened as his scratchy voice croaked on about the Kingfish. Every so often, he would repeat a few words right in the middle of his sentence.

"This place was once full, full of cows. They sailed here years ago, years ago, from a place called Bermooda. Well, one day the

46

Kingfish and his crew, his crew of shellfish, arrive in his ship, the *Tyrant*. They didn't get along, get along too well with the cows. They figured cows ain't got no place on the water. One day, the Kingfish got into it with a big one-eyed bull."

Chuck and Dakota looked at each other. They both had a feeling they knew who the one-eyed bull was. They were starting to understand why Marco and Ribeye didn't want to come into town.

"There was an argument, which turned into a swordfight, and…well, ol' Kingfish lost some whiskers," Nwar said. "After that, the Kingfish and his pirates ran pretty much every cow off the island. He's hated cows, hated cows ever since. So…what are you little cows doing here?"

Marco had said not to tell anyone about

47

their plan. But Chuck was brimming with so much excitement that he looked like he might explode. Before Dakota could stop him, Chuck blurted out, "We're looking for the Coral Crown!" Chuck went on to blabber about the crown, the map, the poem, the hornpipe… *everything*. Dakota just shook his head.

"The Coral Crown, you say? Always thought that was only a legend, a legend, just like them monstrous *hu'mans*. Boy, I bet the ol' Kingfish would love to get his fins on that!" Nwar cawed with a croaky laugh. "Well, best of luck to you, lads. Thanks for letting an old bird talk your ears off." He made a slight bow before flapping out the door.

"Now you've done it!" Dakota said. "Marco said not to tell anyone!"

"He seemed nice," Chuck said. "It's not like I went and told the Kingfish."

48

But no sooner had Chuck uttered those words than the Kingfish himself burst right through the front door.

"Well," Dakota gulped. "Here's your big chance."

The Kingfish was not a king at all, but an enormous catfish. Standing on his tail, he was quite tall—about twice as tall as Chuck and Dakota. He was also rather sloppy, with a round belly that bounced under his chin. He wore a gruesome smile, with two big, oversized front teeth that stuck out past his big, oversized lips. Long whiskers curled out from around his ugly face. On his left side, they could see several short nubs where whiskers used to be. His beady, cat-like eyes were set far apart, covered by thin glasses that stretched across his wide nose. From his head came a pointy fin that looked like a crown.

He spotted Chuck and Dakota almost immediately. He waddled a bit as he strolled across the room toward them on his tail fin. Chuck hid the hornpipe behind his back.

"Well now…what have we here?!" he said in a deep voice. "Cows? On MY island? And runty little cows at that!" He picked Dakota up by the foot with his fin. Dakota did his best to keep his cow mask on as the Kingfish held him upside down and peered at him through his glasses.

"Put my brother down!" Chuck mooed. He ran up and stomped a hoof on the King-fish's tail.

"Ooooh, you're a feisty one!" the Kingfish crooned, grabbing Chuck by the shirt. The Kingfish was quite strong. Chuck and Dakota both dangled from his fins as he began to shake them up and down.

"What do you say there, boys? Anyone want a milkshake?" he teased, letting out a deep belly laugh. The shellfish in the room cackled along with him. But their laughter stopped when they heard a familiar voice yell out:

"*Ora basta!* That's enough!"

Everyone froze as Marco appeared in the doorway. The Kingfish released his grip on Chuck and Dakota. Falling to the floor, they scrambled to the door behind Marco. For a few moments, everything was silent as Marco and the Kingfish stared each other down.

"These cows are sailing under my flag," Marco said. "If you bother them, you are bothering me."

"Pollo!" the Kingfish jeered. "Now, I should've known that you'd be the one to bring two grass-chewers to my island…with that first mate of yours and all. Where is that one-eyed beefsteak you pal around with, Pollo? He and I still got a score to settle."

Marco smirked at the Kingfish. He didn't seem to be afraid, even though he was much smaller. "You should be more careful, my slippery friend," he said. "You might lose the other half of your whiskers. And you know how silly a pirate looks without a beard." Marco had a reputation for being an expert swordsman, and the Kingfish knew it.

The grisly catfish scowled at them for a few moments before grumbling, "I'm gonna let you off with a warning. *Today*. But if you little hamburgers ever show up on my island again...I'll turn your hides into leather." With that, Chuck, Dakota, and Marco backed out of the door.

"What did I tell you?" Marco clucked angrily as they made their way back to the ship. "I told you to *stay away* from-a The Black Spot! I told you to stay away from the Kingfish! *Marco* is the captain here! If you sail on *Marco's* ship, you follow *Marco's* orders! *Capice?*"

Chuck and Dakota looked shamefully down at their feet. "Yes, sir."

Marco sighed. "I knew you cows would be bad luck. We were supposed come and go quietly. Now we have to leave Cattleena right away! All so you can find some silly flute! Did you at least keep quiet about our voyage?"

"Yes, sir," they both lied. With Marco so angry, they were afraid to mention their chat with the black parrot.

Back on the deck of the *Swashclucker*, Chuck and Dakota studied the hornpipe as they sailed away in the night.

"So what does this thing do?" Dakota wondered.

"Makes music, of course," Chuck said. He took the hornpipe and tried to play a song, but his hooves made it difficult to play more than one or two notes.

"Here, you play it," he said, handing it to Dakota. "You have fingers."

Dakota looked at the name of the last song on the list. "Fire in the Heavens," he read. "That sounds pretty cool."

Dakota played the notes on the sheet. As he got to the end of the tune, the hornpipe began to shake. He pulled it away from his mouth as little sparks jumped from inside. Suddenly, a bolt of fire shot out of the hornpipe! The fire arced into the sky, where it exploded like a firecracker. The sound echoed across the water. Dakota's eyes grew big as dinner plates. He very slowly and carefully put down the hornpipe.

"Maybe you should start with the *first* song," Chuck suggested.

"Maybe we should get some sleep," Dakota said.

Below deck, Dakota fell asleep right away. But Chuck lay awake for hours, thinking about the other verses on the map. *A spying eye? Stars of our own?* What did it all mean? He went over the phrases in his head again and again, until the gentle lobbing of the ship finally rocked him to sleep.

WATERDOWN

Chuck and Dakota awoke at dawn to the sound of Marco crowing on the ship's bow. They clambered out of their bunk, rubbing their eyes in the morning light as they came up to the ship's deck.

"*Buon Giorno*, Buccowneers!" Marco crowed. "Rise and shine! Big day ahead of us!"

After a quick breakfast of bananas and corn, Chuck and Dakota took time to experiment with the hornpipe some more while Marco watched. This time, Dakota decided to start with the first song on the list,

"The Fishes' Breath." It was a very short tune with only eight notes. When Dakota played the jaunty little ditty...*BWOP!* A big bubble appeared around him.

Chuck snickered. "You look like you just got burped up by a fish!" he joked. They both laughed as Marco popped the bubble with his sword. They went on like that for a while—Dakota playing the tune and making bubbles, while Marco and Chuck kept popping them and laughing. For a moment, they forgot all about the Kingfish and the trouble they'd gotten into the night before.

Before too long, they heard Ribeye give his "Land Ho!" grunt. They dashed to the railing and looked off the starboard bow to see the tops of several ships' masts sticking out of the water. They reminded Dakota of tombstones.

"*Waterdown*," Marco said, looking through his spyglass. "The final resting place for many a doomed ship. Make a wide circle, Ribeye. Let's not get too close to that graveyard, unless we wish to be part of it."

"Wait! We're just gonna go around? What about the clues?" Chuck pointed to the shipwrecks as he recited the second line of the poem. "*A watery grave where the clock strikes eleven*'. What time is it right now?"

"Nine thirty," Marco answered.

Chuck scratched his chin with a hoof. "Are we supposed to wait until eleven?"

"We do not wait at all!" Marco said. "We sail on to the next place on the map."

"Please, Captain! Can't we explore the shipwrecks?" Chuck pleaded. "It won't take too long! Who knows what kind of treasure there might be?"

Normally, Marco would have no desire to drop anchor here. He would have preferred to go around this shipwreck and head to Sterling Reef. But he had to admit the hornpipe Chuck found was pretty remarkable. And the little calf had a good point: there could be more treasure in this wreck.

"Fine," Marco agreed. "But we do not wait until eleven o'clock. You must look right now."

They couldn't see much of the underwater wreckage from the surface. Chuck thought about the next line of the poem: *"A spying eye sees when our own eyes do fail."* He thought maybe he could see further down through Marco's spyglass. But when he asked, Marco refused.

"No one touches Marco's spyglass," Marco said flatly. "A captain's spyglass is a treasure in itself."

Chuck thought and thought about how to get down underwater. *I'd have to be able to breathe like a fish!* he thought. Suddenly, his tail began to twitch.

"That's it!" he said. "The first song is 'The Fishes' Breath'! We can use that bubble to go underwater!"

"Do you enjoy getting us in trouble?" Dakota asked. "Now you want me to go into an underwater graveyard?" Dakota did not like the idea of underwater danger any more than above-water danger.

"Come on!" Chuck said. "I just know there's something important down there!"

Dakota knew Chuck's plan was going to bring him trouble. But he played "The Fishes' Breath" anyway.

BWOP! The bubble blew up around the both of them. They gently sank into the water, but inside the bubble, they were dry and surrounded by air.

Chuck looked around at the bubble with a sense of wonder. "Isn't this amazing?" he marveled. "We're breathing underwater!"

With a little bit of practice and little bit of teamwork, they found that they could pilot the bubble around in the water by rolling it with their feet. Before long, they were pedaling around in the water with ease. They headed for the shipwrecks.

The wreckage loomed in front of them like a collection of giant, sleeping skeletons. It looked a lot like the *Hortica* on Bermooda, except this was dark and murky and much bigger. Everything was covered in barnacles, seaweed, and green algae. This place had not been disturbed in a long time.

Neither of them were sure where to begin looking. Chuck suggested that they start in the captains' quarters, just like they did on the *Swashclucker*. They pedaled their bubble through a big hole in the roof of the largest ship's cabin.

The inside of the cabin was bare. Dakota scratched his head as they looked around the watery room. There was an old table broken in half, a chandelier without any candles, and a few empty barrels. The windows were all shattered, with stained glass scattered all around. The two of them were about to leave the room when Chuck spotted an old chest in the corner.

"Look!" Chuck said. "Look at the chest. It has a clock on it!" The clock on the chest was smashed and broken. Its hands were stopped at precisely eleven o'clock, and looked as though they had been there for hundreds of years. "This is where the clock strikes eleven!" Chuck was so excited he started clapping his hooves together.

Dakota pulled the cow mask away from his face. For once, he was amazed. "Are we supposed to take the broken clock?" he asked.

"I think we're supposed to take whatever's in that chest." Chuck said. The front of the chest had rotted away, and they could see something was inside. When they pedaled the bubble closer, they made out the shape of a spyglass covered in slimy green gunk.

"*A spying eye!*" Chuck gasped. "Let's reach in and get it!"

"That thing?" Dakota said. "It's all gross. Besides, Marco already has a spyglass."

"You heard what Marco said," Chuck reminded him. "A captain's spyglass is a treasure in itself."

Chuck reached out toward the chest. He froze as his hoof neared the edge of the bubble. "Uh-oh," he muttered. He suddenly realized that there was one thing they had to do before grabbing their new treasure. "We have to pop the bubble!"

"What about our air?" Dakota said, as all the color drained from his face.

"Just take a deep breath," Chuck said. "As soon as I grab that spyglass, play the song again so we can get our bubble back."

Dakota's hands shook as Chuck's plan got more dangerous by the minute. They both took a deep breath, Dakota held the pointy end of the hornpipe to the side of the bubble, and…*POP!*

The first thing Dakota noticed was how surprisingly cold the water was. It rushed in from everywhere, making all his muscles tense up. Chuck reached out quickly and broke his hoof through the rotten wood of the chest. He grabbed the spyglass and nodded his head at Dakota. Dakota put the hornpipe to his lips and blew hard into the hornpipe, playing "The Fishes' Breath."

BLOOP! BLIP! BLOOP! All that came out were air bubbles! Chuck closed his eyes as he realized the flaw in his plan: You can't play a hornpipe underwater!

Dakota flailed his arms and legs in a panic. He had used up all his air blowing into the hornpipe. The cold water squeezed him from all sides as he began to sink.

Chuck grabbed Dakota by the shirt and swam up and out of the cabin. Cows were known for having strong legs, but Chuck knew that even legs as strong as his wouldn't take them all the way to the surface. Instead, he started kicking toward the anchor chain for the *Swashclucker*, dragging Dakota with him. They both grabbed onto the chain and started climbing and kicking as quickly as they could, leaving a trail of bubbles behind them. The water got warmer as they neared the ocean surface, until… *SPLASH!* Their heads popped out of the waves about ten feet away from the *Swashclucker*.

Dakota and Chuck gasped for air, taking in big, hungry breaths as they clung to the anchor chain. They were very tired but very excited they survived and they couldn't wait to look at their new treasure. But before they could even look through their new spyglass, a huge shadow covered both them and the *Swashclucker*. It was the large shadow of a large ship speeding up right up alongside them.

Their secret voyage was no longer a secret. They were not alone.

THE TYRANT

Ribeye helped Chuck and Dakota climb back up onto the *Swashclucker*.

"It's about time!" Marco crowed. "We have company!"

"Who is that?" Dakota asked, still catching his breath.

"That's the *Tyrant*! The Kingfish's ship!" Marco said. "I told you to stay away from him!"

Dakota's face fell. "That's the *Tyrant*?" he squealed.

The Tyrant was much bigger than the

Swashclucker. It was more than twice as long, and was outfitted with cannons all down the side. Big, scary spikes stuck up from its deck and an enormous fish skull stuck out from its bow. It had raggedy sails and a flag as red as blood blew in the breeze.

Worst of all, the *Tyrant* was loaded with ferocious shellfish—dozens of them, far more than they had seen in the Black Spot. Lobsters, crayfish, cannibal shrimp, and all kinds of crabs littered the deck and masts of the *Tyrant*, gnashing their claws and whipping their antennae. As they pulled up alongside the *Swashclucker*, a gang of crayfish jumped across to their mast.

"What are they doing?" Chuck mooed.

"They're *pirates*, you *kau'pai*!" Dakota cried. "They're attacking us!"

The crayfish began coming down the ship's

lines. At the same time, a troop of crabs began climbing over the side of the ship, scuttling onto the deck.

"They're overtaking the ship!" Marco shouted, drawing his sword. "I hope whatever you found in that-a shipwreck was worth it!"

Chuck held up the slimy, grungy telescope.

"That's it?" Marco clucked. "A spyglass? I already have a spyglass!"

Chuck's shoulders slumped. As a great explorer, he thought for sure that Marco would be more excited.

The pirates set a plank across the two ships. A brigade of burly lobsters marched across the bridge, followed by none other than the Kingfish himself. Chuck and Dakota looked right at him as he strolled aboard the *Swashclucker*, and he looked right back at them as they held the hornpipe and spyglass.

"*Andare!* Scram!" Marco ordered the calves. "Go hide in the cabin! Ribeye and I will fight them off!"

Chuck and Dakota followed the captain's orders, scurrying into Marco's cabin and locking the door.

"Oh, no!" Chuck mooed. "The Kingfish saw the spyglass!"

"Who cares? What are *we* gonna do?" Dakota panicked.

"I'll think of something!" Chuck said as he looked around the room for an idea. The door banged loudly as shellfish pirates tried to break their way into the cabin. Suddenly, Chuck's gaze landed on Marco's spyglass.

"I've got it!" he said. He quickly rolled the old spyglass in a rug and stashed it in a trash barrel in the corner of the cabin. Then he grabbed Marco's spyglass from the table. It was very fancy. Tiny diamonds were embedded in its rich wood. It had gold rims and a gold eyepiece. It was heavy and shiny and sparkly… and looked every bit like a treasure.

No sooner had Chuck taken Marco's spyglass in his hand than two big crayfish burst their way into the door. The crayfish dragged Chuck and Dakota out of the cabin and up to the quarterdeck, where the Kingfish already had Marco and Ribeye held prisoner by six heavily armed lobsters. They had put up a glorious fight, but they were no match for an entire pirate army. The crew of the *Swashclucker* watched helplessly from the ship's wheel as shellfish began stealing whatever they could find on the ship.

"A prisoner on my own ship," Marco grumbled. "You calves are definitely bad luck."

"Some treasure hunt," Dakota murmured.

"How did you find us?" Chuck asked the Kingfish.

Dakota frowned as a familiar black parrot fluttered down and perched on the Kingfish's shoulder. "I'm guessing a little bird told him."

"Nwar!" Chuck mooed. "You rotten spy!"

Marco gave Chuck a look as sharp as daggers. "You said you didn't tell anyone!" he clucked.

"Okay, so I told the parrot!" Chuck admitted. "But I didn't think he'd *repeat* it!"

Marco's beak dropped open. "That's what parrots DO!"

"I told you I'd let you off with a warning for one day," The Kingfish said with an evil grin. "Well, that was yesterday. Today's a new day, and I woke up feeling a whole lot less generous." He motioned his head to the parrot on his shoulder. "My friend here tells me you're on your way to find the Coral Crown. Says you've got a map and everything. Now, you do know that only a king should wear a crown, right?"

Ribeye answered the Kingfish with a series of snorts and grunts, all the while giving him the stink-eye.

"Don't worry, Cyclops," the Kingfish said with a cruel smile. "I'll get to you in a minute. But first…I want that map. And I want that flute. And I want whatever you just took out of that shipwreck."

"We'll give you nothing, you shovel-nosed bottom-feeder!" Marco clucked boldly.

"You talk big, Pollo," the Kingfish taunted. "But you can't fight off all of us. In the end, it looks you're nothing but a scrawny…little… *chicken*."

Marco didn't care for the way the Kingfish

had said the word "chicken". It sounded an awful lot like he was comparing chickens with weaklings and cowards. He tried to break free again, but the lobsters holding him were too strong. The entire ship of shellfish roared with laughter.

"You field-trotters just don't get it, do you?" the Kingfish jeered. "I'm the boss around here. I'm the king. You don't belong here. This is a fish's ocean. It's *my* ocean. That means everything in it also belongs…to *me*." He stretched out a fin and snatched Marco's spyglass from Chuck's hooves.

"Hey! That's my spyglass!" Marco squawked.

"Well, now it's my *spyglass*," the Kingfish gloated. "Now give me that flute thing you took from my tavern."

Nwar flapped over to Dakota and tried to take the hornpipe. Dakota refused to hand it over, and the two of them wrestled back and forth over it. Nwar cleverly molted a cluster of black feathers right in Dakota's face, and Dakota dropped the hornpipe. The sly parrot carried it in his beak and dropped it in the Kingfish's fin.

"So what's the big deal with this little thing?" the Kingfish asked.

Chuck's tail began to twitch as a great idea came into his head.

"Well…it plays music," he answered. "Perfect entertainment for those long, boring sea voyages." He gave Dakota a sideways glance. "In fact, Dakota here can play a *heavenly* song for you that will just set the place on *fire*. How about it, your highness? Can we play one *last* song?"

Dakota felt his heart beat faster as he realized Chuck's plan. The Kingfish shrugged

77

his fins and tossed the hornpipe back to Dakota. "Go on, little hamburger. Entertain me."

Chuck watched nervously as Dakota played the last song on the list, "Fire in the Heavens." Just as before, the hornpipe started jumping and bumping when he finished the tune. Dakota aimed the hornpipe toward the *Tyrant* as sparks spewed from inside. Once again, a bolt of fire shot out, streaking like a comet straight to the Kingfish's ship. It exploded in flames, lighting his sails ablaze.

"My sails! My ship!" the Kingfish shrieked. He roared at his crew in a panic. "Move it, you swabs! Put the fire out!"

Shellfish everywhere began to scramble, scurrying back to the *Tyrant* as the Kingfish screamed orders from the *Swashclucker*'s quarterdeck. In all the commotion, Marco broke free. He flapped up to the ship's yardarm and pulled on the lines, unfurling the *Swashclucker*'s main sail. It billowed in the wind, swinging the ship's heavy wooden boom across the quarterdeck and knocking the Kingfish and his goons right into the water.

"Hoist the anchor!" Marco ordered as he flapped to the ship's wheel.

"Stop them! Stop them!" the Kingfish blubbered as he searched for his glasses in the water. By this time, the Kingfish's crew realized they had been tricked. Three big coconut crabs started rushing their way back to the *Swashclucker* with their powerful claws snapping.

"Never mind!" Marco squawked. "CUT the anchor!"

Ribeye unhooked the anchor's chain from the ship. The chain disappeared into the water as the *Swashclucker* swiftly took off in the strong tropical wind.

"*Ciao*, your majesty!" Marco crowed back at the Kingfish with a phony bow. "We'll send you a postcard from-a Spidercrab Rock!"

The Kingfish was furious. But with his ship's sails on fire and his crew in a panic, there was nothing he could do but watch them escape. He ranted and raved from his spot in the water, watching the *Swashclucker* get smaller and smaller until it disappeared on the horizon.

7
LULLABY

With the Kingfish far behind them, the *Swashclucker* and the crew were well on their way to Sterling Reef. But not everyone was as happy as they should have been.

Marco paced his cabin in frustration. His map was no longer a secret, his ship had been looted, and he had lost his spyglass to the Kingfish. *These two calves are bringing me nothing but trouble*, he thought. *If it weren't for my quick thinking, we never would have escaped!*

Marco wasn't the only one in a foul mood. Dakota spent much of the day moping and thinking about all the fun and *safe* things he could be doing back on Bermooda.

Chuck tried to pull Dakota out of his funk by reading the poem from map aloud.

"What about this last line?" Chuck nudged Dakota's shoulder. "*'Those who bring ruin will earn it as well.'* What do you think that means?"

Dakota pretended to ignore Chuck as he tossed a pebble into the water. He looked out at the sea, which glittered like gold as the late afternoon's sunbeams danced across it. *I could be laying in a hammock right now,* he thought.

"*I* think it means that you get what you give," Chuck went on. "Bullies like the Kingfish? They get what they deserve."

Dakota scoffed. "Bullies *never* get what they deserve. I know what bullies are like. The orphanage I ran away from was full of them. Bullies take whatever they want. They take your lunch. They take your bed. They push you around. And they always get away with it."

Marco came out from his cabin, interrupting them. "We should be upon Sterling Reef soon. If I had my spyglass, I could keep a lookout for it. I can't believe it's in the fins of that slimy, whiskered pirate!"

"It's okay, Captain," Chuck held up the spyglass he found in the shipwreck. "We have *this* one!" Chuck had done his best to clean all the gunk and barnacles from the old spyglass. Underneath all the muck, he found it had a rough wooden finish with a pattern of curly waves carved into the side.

Marco was still not impressed. His spyglass was much shinier and prettier than this old thing. He frowned as he inspected the telescope. It seemed to work just fine, even though it was so ancient. But he couldn't see anything special about it.

"It works," Marco said. "But it's-a nowhere near as-a useful as that flute of yours. What else can-a that thing do besides blow bubbles and shoot fire?"

"Well, I haven't played this song yet," Dakota said. He began to play "Tempest and the Tide." It was a spooky-sounding tune, with lots of eerie flat notes. As he played, the clouds darkened and gathered above them. The breeze strengthened into a strong wind, and the sea around them began to swell and rise.

Chuck clamped a hoof over the hornpipe. "Okay, stop. Maybe we should save that one for later."

"I don't believe I've ever seen a cow play the flute so well. You manage nicely with those

hooves," Marco said, looking at the coconut
shells that disguised Dakota's human hands.

"Oh, ummm…you must have learned how
to do that when you were growing up on your
boat…right, Dakota?" Chuck stammered.

Chuck and Dakota explained to Marco that
Dakota was a "Sea Cow," who had once lived
on a boat with his family. They told him the tale

of how his family became lost at sea while he was visiting Bermooda, making him an orphan.

None of that was true, of course. Dakota was an orphan, but never had a real family that he could remember. That story, much like his cowmouflage, was just another made-up disguise to hide the fact that he was a hu'man.

It always bothered Dakota a little to tell this lie. But Chuck insisted that they keep his identity a secret, and Dakota figured if Marco was in the habit of making up stories, he shouldn't feel too guilty about doing the same thing.

Chuck glanced at the sheet music. "'Song o' the Sea Cow'," he read aloud. "What does that one sound like?"

Dakota took a deep breath and played "Song o' the Sea Cow." It was sweet and soothing, like a lullaby. All four shipmates felt a wave of sleepiness wash over them as Dakota played its gentle tones. Their heads began to swim as they fell under the spell of the hornpipe's lullaby. Marco forgot all about his bad luck. Ribeye smiled for the fist time ever. All their troubles seemed to float away as the gentle melody covered them like a warm blanket. Soon, all four of them were fast asleep. As sunset neared, the *Swashclucker* sailed on toward Sterling Reef, with no one awake…and no one behind the wheel.

8

THE SILVER COWS

The *Swashclucker* crew awoke to a loud crunch and a sudden lurch. They slid across the deck as everything tilted to the side. The ship made a groaning noise as it came to a complete stop.

"What happened?" Dakota asked. "Did we all fall *asleep*?"

Chuck rubbed his eyes and looked over the ship's railing. Below was a giant ring of shallow coral with a lush, green lagoon in the center. The *Swashclucker* was perched on the edge of it. They had crashed right into Sterling Reef.

They rushed below deck, looking for damage. Sure enough, the reef had gouged a hole in the hull. They wouldn't be able to put the *Swashclucker* back in the water without fixing it. Marco buried his face in his wings. Just when he thought everything was going so well!

Chuck peeked through the hole to the outside. "It's not that bad…" he began. He stopped short when a face popped up on the other side of the hole. A cow face. A *silver* cow face.

"Silver cow! Silver cow!" he babbled, pointing at the hole. The face disappeared. Without thinking, Chuck dove into the hole after it. He fell through, landing in the shallow water on the other side. His shipmates joined him as he pulled himself up, and they found themselves face-to-face with a shiny cow bobbing in the waves.

"The Silver Cow from our ghost hunt!" Dakota said. "It's real!"

This cow was clearly not a ghost. It was unlike any cow they'd ever seen. It had flippers instead of hooves. Its fur glinted like metal and its big round fish eyes gleamed like glass. It was singing the same sweet melody that Dakota had played on the hornpipe. But the most shocking thing was yet to come. When the silver cow dove under the water, they saw that it had the tail of a fish!

"It's a Mana Ti'i," Marco whispered, removing his hat. "Legend says they arise at sunset and sing their beautiful song all through the night. I have never seen one with my own eyes until now." He smiled at Dakota. "You may have come from the ocean, my friend. But these…are the *real* Sea Cows."

They gazed around in amazement.

Hundreds of singing Mana Ti'i covered the reef. They all glittered in the light of the setting sun, making the whole coral reef shine like a silver ring on the water.

Then something caught Chuck's attention. In the middle of all that silver, the low tide had exposed a rock that flashed gold in the center of the lagoon.

"What's that? It looks like gold!" Chuck twitched his tail and flared his nostrils,

convinced this was another clue. He charged out into the shallow water.

"Wait!" Dakota called out. But Chuck was already splashing his way furiously toward the shimmering rock. Dakota, Marco, and Ribeye set off after him, tromping through the water. They caught up just as Chuck crawled up to a ledge of the rock. They now saw the gold came from a large key embedded into the side of the coral.

"A key! It's a key!" Chuck panted. "Look! It's made of gold coral! Just like the crown!" Chuck's hooves shook as they eagerly chipped away at the rock until the key came loose. "Coral Crown, coral key...it all makes sense! It's *'a key of her kind!'*"

Then a soft voice came from above, "Why do you seek the Coral Crown?"

Startled, they all snapped their heads up to find a Sea Cow perched majestically on top of the rock. She wore a crown of lotus flowers and had eyes that seemed to be full of sadness.

"I am Lyra," she said. They were all hypnotized by her voice, which rang like jingling bells. "Why do you seek the Coral Crown?" she repeated.

"My family has-a sought that prize for generations," Marco said proudly. "My grandfather, my great grandfather, my great-great grandfather, my great uncle, my third-a cousin on my mother's side…"

"Do you know what the crown is?" she gently interrupted.

Dakota expected Marco to launch into another tale, but surprisingly Marco clucked not a word. It was his turn to hear a story.

"Long before cows or chickens sailed the sea, a beast with an unstoppable appetite threatened to devour the entire ocean. The eleven noble creatures of the sea—the Dolphin, the Octopus, the Whale, the Crab, the Sea Turtle, the Stingray, the Marlin, the Hammerhead, the Seal, the Squid, and the Starfish—joined together. They crafted the crown from gold coral—coral from the deepest and most beautiful parts of the ocean. The noble hearts of the crown's creators gave it a magical power that even the beast could not stand up against. The beast became powerless in the crown's presence, and was no longer able to destroy the ocean. Peace returned to the sea.

The noble creatures then locked the crown away in a secret, guarded place where it protects the sea to this day. However, the Starfish wrote its location in the sky, hidden in a constellation shaped like a crown.

The crown is not a prize, my dear sailors. Whoever wears the crown...holds the heart of the Cowibbean Sea."

"I wish *I* could wear the crown," Dakota muttered. "I'd show that bully Kingfish a thing or two."

"I'm not sure anyone should wear the crown," Lyra said. "The crown brings your heart's desires to life. Is anyone's heart that pure?"

Chuck felt his face suddenly flush. "OH, NO!" he cried. "I told that parrot everything! Every single stop on the map! Can you imagine what will happen if the Kingfish gets the crown first? His heart is full of nothing but hate!"

"His heart is full of fear," Lyra's jingly voice rang. "The things we choose to hate are often those that we fear. Even the fiercest bully has something of which he is afraid."

Dakota had a hard time imagining anything that could frighten the Kingfish.

"You seem to have noble hearts, little calves," Lyra sang. "If your desire is to stop the Kingfish, then this key is yours. But be sure to guard your own hearts well."

Chuck took the key in his hooves. "*Moohalo*," he thanked her.

The four shipmates spent much of their night patching the hole in the *Swashclucker*. They were tired, but too excited to sleep. They all laid on the ship's deck, listening to the waves break against the reef.

"Ten brave roosters of my family have all searched for the prize and failed," Marco sighed. "Now I think perhaps it is because a prize is all they saw."

A troublesome thought crossed Dakota's mind as he thought back to Lyra's story. "The beast...do you suppose it was a hu'man?"

"Ha HA!" Marco cackled. "Little cow, I've seen horrific monsters from the darkest depths of the sea. But *hu'mans*? That would be truly unbelievable."

Chuck turned the coral key over in his hooves, admiring the way it sparkled in the moonlight. "The poem says *'we shall be guided by stars of our own'*," he said. "Marco, have you ever seen a constellation in the shape of a crown?"

"Never," Marco shook his head. "And I've used the stars as a guide all my life. But we already know where the crown is. It's at Spidercrab Rock." Marco slid his hat down over his face. "It's just an old song," he yawned. "No one can *make* stars."

Now ready for bed, Chuck and Dakota went to their bunk and found that the Kingfish's pirates had taken all their blankets during the raid. But the night was warm and the Sea Cows were singing again. Before long, they were lulled into a well-earned sleep.

9

THE TEMPEST

Chuck and Dakota awoke at dawn to the sound of Marco's crowing once again. Arriving on deck, they were greeted by a bright red sky.

"Red sky at morning," Dakota said. "Doesn't that mean a storm is coming?"

"That is the least of our worries!" Marco said. "We have bigger problems coming!"

They squinted into the sunrise and saw the *Tyrant* headed their way, sailing along at full speed. The Kingfish had caught up with them. As the ship neared, they saw the burnt sails had been repaired with some very familiar-looking material.

"Hey!" Dakota cried. "Those are our blankets, you pirates!"

At the sight of the *Tyrant*, all the Mana Ti'i dove into the water, hiding beneath the waves. But the Kingfish wasn't coming to the reef. Instead, the *Tyrant* glided by.

"What's he doing?" Dakota wondered.

"He's passing us!" Marco realized.

"He's going to beat us to the crown!" Chuck looked down at the *Swashclucker*'s keel, still resting on the coral. "We have to get off this reef! If only the tide were higher!"

Dakota's mind zipped back to the day before, when he made the skies darken and the waters rise by playing the hornpipe. He grabbed the flute and the sheet music.

"Everybody hold on!" he warned. Taking a

100

deep breath, he began playing "Tempest and the Tide." A low rumble filled the skies above. Puffy gray clouds began to fill the morning sky. The wind began to blow harder. The water began to rise.

"Not enough!" Chuck mooed, looking down at the reef. "Play louder! Play faster!"

Dakota played louder and faster. The clouds thickened, blocking out the red sunrise as he repeated the song over and over. The water rose higher and higher, lifting them off the reef. The wind, which now gusted so hard they had to yell to be heard, carried them swiftly after the *Tyrant*.

Ribeye tied down the sails. Marco flapped up to the crow's nest to get a better look at the Tyrant.

"We're catching up!" Marco crowed. He pointed at Chuck and yelled, "Steer!"

"Me?" Chuck yelled back. "I'm not a steer! I'm just a calf!"

"No, you silly cow!" Marco clucked wildly, pointing ahead to the Tyrant. "STEER!"

Chuck got on the ship's wheel and did his best to steer. But the weather was getting out of control. The sky had turned almost black. Rain poured down in buckets. Both the *Swashclucker* and the *Tyrant* were getting slammed by waves that pounded the ships' hulls.

"*Basta!*" Marco squawked to Dakota. "*Stop!* Stop playing!"

But the storm couldn't be stopped. It was now a full-blown tempest, with wind and waves that tossed both ships around on the sea like toys in a bathtub. Soon, neither ship could see the other through the driving rain and the waves crashing over the deck. Ribeye took over the wheel as lightning ripped through the dark sky. The *Swashclucker* turned on its side in the wind, knocking everyone onto their faces. The key bounced out of Chuck's shirt pocket and skittered off the ship into the water.

"The key!" Chuck shrieked. But in the shake of a cow's tail, Dakota leapt into the raging sea with the hornpipe in his hand. He grabbed the key before it could sink. Fighting to keep his head above water, he then played the notes for "The Fishes' Breath."

BWOP! A bubble appeared around Dakota and the key. The waves bounced him like a beach ball before picking him up and slamming him upside-down into the water near the *Swashclucker*. The bubble broke, leaving Dakota with his head underwater. Ribeye grasped Dakota's feet and pulled him aboard just as a colossal wave hurled the ship up into the air. Dakota's stomach churned as the wall of water sent the ship crashing down again. The black sky swirled in front of Dakota's eyes as the *Swashclucker* spun out of control…then everything went black for him, too.

10

SPIDER CRAB ROCK

Dakota awoke to Chuck's face hovering over him.

"Hey, you're awake!" he mooed. "You've been out for over thirty minutes."

They had weathered the storm. The sea was now calm, and the *Tyrant* was nowhere in sight.

Dakota sat and rubbed the back of his head. "Where are we?" he asked.

"The storm a-threw us off," Marco called out form the ship's wheel. "But not terribly so. I have-a nearly managed to get us a-back on course. And I did it all without that grubby old spyglass."

"That was pretty brave for someone who doesn't even believe the crown exists," Chuck said, helping Dakota to his feet.

Dakota handed over the key. "I don't know what I believe anymore. I just couldn't let that Kingfish win."

They sailed on. But after a few hours they began to feel like they were going in circles. Marco checked and double-checked the map, then sat down in confusion.

"I don't-a understand," Marco took off his hat and scratched his head. "This should-a be the right place."

"Maybe the storm blew us further off course than we thought," Chuck said.

"Impossible!" Marco said. "According to the map, Spidercrab Rock should be right there!" He pointed to an empty spot about a half-mile away.

"So…what, then? It just doesn't exist?" Dakota asked. Marco remained silent. He had no more answers.

"Great!" Dakota shouted, throwing his hands in the air. "I just knew it! There is no Spidercrab Rock! There is no Coral Crown! We came all this way for nothing!"

Chuck felt crushed. He wiped the lens of the old spyglass and peered through, hoping he'd find something to prove their whole mission had not been a waste.

"Just when I started to believe!" Dakota continued, letting his temper fly. "Some adventure! Some treasure hunt! It's all just another stupid fairy tale!"

"No…it's not!" Chuck's eyes went wild and his jaw went slack. He held out the spyglass and pointed ahead. "Look! LOOK!"

Marco snatched the spyglass. Squinting through its grimy lens, he saw exactly what Chuck had just seen. Spidercrab Rock was right in front of them.

"Mamma mia!" Marco gasped. He pulled the spyglass away and rubbed his eyes in disbelief. "The island is invisible!"

Now they understood why this crusty old thing was so special. Only through its magical lens could they actually see Spidercrab Rock. Without the spyglass…nothing. Through the spyglass…island!

"*'A spying eye sees when our own eyes do fail,'*" Chuck recited the poem.

"*'Into the nothingness…BRAVELY WE SAIL!'*" Marco crowed, finishing the line. He fluttered up to the top of the mast. "Onward, buccowneers! Ha ha ha! I knew you little cows would bring good luck!"

Ribeye piloted the *Swashclucker* into the nothingness. Had anyone been watching, they would have seen the ship suddenly vanish into thin air. All at once, the crew found themselves surrounded by a glittering blue fog on the water. They could now clearly see the island without the spyglass, although no one on the outside could see them. As long as they were inside this magical mist, they were invisible.

Marco molted feathers with excitement as they glided toward Spidercrab Rock. The island rose high up out of the water like a giant boulder, and was chiseled into a colossal temple that towered above them. Two sparkling waterfalls poured from the sides of the rock, cascading down into the sea.

Chuck wrinkled his brow. "Why is it called Spidercrab Rock? It doesn't look anything like a spider crab. They should have called it 'Weeping Rock'. Those waterfalls make it look like the rock is crying."

Carved at the top of temple was the same pattern of curly waves that was on the spyglass, along with the shape of a crown. They all agreed that the Coral Crown must be inside.

"How do we get in?" Dakota asked. The

temple had no doors or windows, just four steep sides and a flat top.

"It looks like the only way in is through there," Marco pointed to a small cave at the base of the island beneath the temple. "But it's too small, even for a rowboat."

"We can use a bubble!" Chuck said. "Dakota, play 'The Fishes' Breath'!"

Dakota felt his belly quiver nervously as if it were full of goldfish. As Ribeye steered the *Swashclucker* closer to the cliff, ripples began to disturb the water. The whole ship began to shimmy and shake. The water between them and the cave began to bubble as though it were boiling.

Then, out of the simmering water rose a monstrous spider crab. He was even bigger than the *Swashclucker*! His long legs were like tree trunks, and his eyes were the size

▌▌▌

of melons. He loomed over the ship with claws that looked as though they could crush through stone.

"Oh…" Chuck said, "that's why it's called Spidercrab Rock."

The enormous crab blocked the entrance to the cave, flexing his legs and snapping his claws.

"Another shellfish!" Marco clucked. "Stay here, little ones! Marco shall-a slay this beast!" He immediately flapped off toward the crab, swinging his sword and crowing furiously. But he was no match for the beast, who swatted at Marco with a monstrous leg. Marco spiraled down into the water with a splash. But the crab didn't attack any further. He just stood between them and the cave, silently waiting for his next challenger.

Marco emerged from the water. He was

sopping wet, hopping mad, and ready to take a second stab at the beast.

"WAIT!" Chuck yelled. "Stop! He won't attack you if you don't attack him!"

But it was no use. Ribeye had already leapt from the ship onto one of the crab's legs, and Marco was already trying to poke holes at him. The crab thrashed his legs around, trying to shake them off.

Chuck quickly ran through the poem in his head. His tail twitched as he looked for their next clue. "I've got it! '*The beast shall sleep at the Sea Cows' song.*' We have to make him sleep!"

"But the Mana Ti'i don't sing until sunset!" Dakota argued. "It's not even noon yet!"

Chuck recalled how they'd fallen asleep when Dakota played the hornpipe. "'Song o' the Sea Cow'! Play 'Song o' the Sea Cow'!" Chuck squealed.

The giant crab now gripped both Marco and Ribeye in his massive claws.

"Cover your ears!" Chuck told them all. "Play, Sea Cow! Play!"

They covered their ears as Dakota played the familiar lullaby. As its calming notes filled the air, the giant crab relaxed his grip on Marco and Ribeye. He wobbled on his legs for a few minutes. He dropped Ribeye and Marco as he sank into slumber on the water.

Ribeye swam back to the ship with Marco perched on his head. "Serves him right, that beast," Marco said as he climbed in and shook the water off his feathers.

"He's not a beast. He's just a guard," Chuck said. "He's making sure no one finds the crown who isn't supposed to."

"Who's going to find it?" Dakota pointed out. "The whole island is invisible."

"Ribeye, guard the *Swashclucker*," Marco ordered, wringing the water from his hat. "We're going in."

Dakota played a few quick notes and a bubble surrounded him, Chuck, and Marco. Ribeye watched from the ship's wheel as they plopped into the water and disappeared into the dark cave. He didn't notice a familiar black parrot creeping out from the *Swashclucker*'s cargo hold, where he'd been hiding since Waterdown. No one saw the spying bird quietly fly off into the mist to find his master, the Kingfish.

Chuck, Dakota, and Marco pedaled their bubble deeper into the darkness. They could see nothing but a tiny dot of light at the cave's mouth. The end of the cave caught them quite by surprise, bursting their bubble against a rocky wall and plunging all three of them into the water.

"Marco?" Chuck blindly splashed around in the dark. "Marco?"

"I'm here," Marco's voice echoed in the dark. "But I'm not too fond of swimming. Someone light the torch."

There was an awkward silence. "No one brought a torch?" Marco scolded.

"I could make some light," Dakota said. He put the hornpipe to his lips. It was too dark to see any sheet music, but having played "Fire in the Heavens" twice already, he did the best he could from memory. Dakota felt the hornpipe shimmy and shake in his hands. He pointed it straight up as the fire trail shot out again…but this time, something different happened. The flames collided with the ceiling and stretched out in all directions. A ribbon of fire ran across the rocks overhead, bathing everything in a warm light. When they looked up, they saw a large granite dome over their heads, spanned by a sea of burning stars.

"Wow!" Dakota said. "We made stars! 'Stars of our own'!"

Everywhere they looked, dozens of stars glowed above and around them like constellations made of fire. Directly overhead, in the tallest part of the dome, were eleven bright stars arranged in the shape of a crown.

"Look!" Chuck pointed. "A crown constellation! A crownstellation!"

The three of them stared up at the ceiling with no idea what to do next. The next line of the poem told them to "reach for the skies". Chuck reached up his arms, but the dome was very high and he was still trying to tread water.

We need the tide to be higher," Dakota said in a hollow voice. They all looked at the hornpipe, knowing what had to be done. The last time they played "Tempest and the Tide," they whipped up a typhoon. Should they play it again?

"Lightly, Sea Cow," Marco said. "Play lightly."

Dakota played very lightly. A whirling breeze swirled through the cave. The water rose slowly, bringing them higher and higher. The closer they got to the crown constellation, the brighter its stars glowed. But that wasn't the only thing that was glowing. The coral key in Chuck's pocket was shimmering brighter and brighter as they neared the top.

Kicking with his feet, Chuck reached up and held the glowing key to the ceiling as they approached the crownstellation. He breathed in sharply, unsure of what was about to happen as the tip of the key hovered inches from the dome.

"Get ready," he said, squeezing his eyes shut. He touched the key to the ceiling. Sparks flew, flames spurted, and a glowing portal of light opened up above their heads. All of a sudden, the three of them felt themselves being stretched like taffy as the portal began pulling them upward. It sucked them up faster and faster into the blinding tunnel of light. A rushing noise like a thousand crashing waves filled their ears, and a fierce wind blew against them.

"Where is it taking us?" Dakota screamed into the deafening noise. Then, just as suddenly as it had started, everything became still and quiet.

Chuck peeked his eyes open. They were laying on a small, flat ledge of marble. Above them was the open sky. Below them he could see the water, the *Swashclucker*, and even the giant crab…still sleeping like a baby.

"We're at the top of the tower!" Chuck said. "The crown isn't IN the temple. It's ON the temple!"

In front of them was a giant clamshell with a keyhole on the front. Carvings of the eleven noble creatures decorated the top of the clamshell.

"Look!" Dakota gasped. "It's all the noble creatures! Just like Lyra told us!"

Light streamed from the keyhole in the clamshell as the key in Chuck's hooves jumped and dipped with a mind of its own.

"This is it!" Marco crowed. "At long last! The Coral Crown! Open it! Open it!"

They put the key into the keyhole, and… nothing! It refused to turn.

"The key won't turn!" Marco squawked. "Why won't the key turn?"

Chuck searched his brain for a clue, but was interrupted by a loud THOOM! from below.

"What was that?" Dakota asked, jerking his head down toward the water. Every muscle in his body tensed as they watched the Tyrant emerge through the mist.

"The Kingfish!" Chuck wailed. "How did he find us?"

They heard another THOOM! as a blast shot out from one of the Tyrant's cannons, followed by a chunk of the temple being smashed away.

"Hey! Are they shooting at us?" Dakota said.

"They're pirates, you kau'pai!" Chuck snapped.

CROWN OF THE COWIBBEAN

The Kingfish's pirates started their attack immediately. The spider crab, who had been sleeping peacefully, awoke angrier than ever at the sound of the *Tyrant*'s cannon. He thrashed and gnashed, defending the cave. Dozens of prawn scuttled all over the spider crab, chomping at him with their own claws. Ribeye drew his sword as a cluster of hard-shelled lobsters climbed aboard the *Swashclucker*.

"Keep working on that clamshell!" Marco ordered. "We'll take care of everything below!" He fluttered down to the battle.

Down below, the spider crab threw shellfish left and right. Ribeye faced off with the lobsters on the *Swashclucker*'s deck. Marco flapped around the crayfish who were working the *Tyrant*'s cannons, making it impossible for them to see what they were doing.

The Kingfish, however, cared nothing about Marco, or Ribeye, or even the spider crab. While everyone was fighting, he climbed the tallest mast of the *Tyrant*, using it to reach the bottom of the temple. He grasped the sides of the temple with his fins, shimmying his way up. His eyes looked wide and crazy, and his whiskers curled and wiggled like snakes coming from his chin. Chuck's and Dakota's eyes got bigger and bigger with fear as the vile catfish flopped his way higher and higher. For a fat, sloppy fish, he was very good at climbing a wall.

Rushing back to the clamshell, they pulled and tugged and jiggled the key, but it still wouldn't turn.

Dakota pounded his fist on the clamshell. "What do we do? There's no hornpipe song for this!"

They heard a crashing sound below as the spider crab splintered one of the *Tyrant*'s masts. He started smashing both ships with his enormous legs.

"The poem says the crown will *'sing to a key of her kind.'*" Chuck thought frantically. "Maybe...maybe...we're supposed to...sing?"

Dakota did a double take. "Sing? Now? Sing what?"

"The poem! What about the poem?" Chuck mooed. "Sing that!"

Dakota cleared his throat. Chuck took a deep breath. Trying to remember the words as best as they could, they sang together:

"Circle of darkness, horn of the heavens,
A watery grave where the clock strikes eleven."

The key began to glow brighter in the lock. For a few moments, it felt like time slowed down. The crown, the crab, the cannons, the Kingfish—everything seemed to happen at once in slow-motion.

"A spying eye sees when our own eyes do fail,
Into the nothingness, bravely we sail."

"Get ready, sweet little hamburgers! I'm coming for you!" the Kingfish yelled from below. The spider crab spotted the Kingfish and began climbing the temple wall after him.

"The beast shall sleep at the Sea-Cows' song,
And we shall be guided by stars of our own."

Ribeye knocked three lobsters into the water, as a dozen more jumped onto the ship.

"Whatever you're doing, do it quickly!" Marco squawked from below. "We cannot hold them much longer!"

"Reach for the skies and a sea rover finds
The crown she doth sing to a key of her kind."

Another cannonball rocketed into the side of the temple as the pirates fired at the spider crab. The spider crab roared. The Kingfish cackled as he neared the top of the temple.

"And guard thy heart, hearties, where wishes do dwell,
For those who bring ruin shall earn it as well."

As their song finished, the key turned itself in the lock…and the shell opened.

"Peek-a-booooooo!!!" the Kingfish sang as his head popped up into view. But just as he appeared, a blinding light shined from the clamshell.

Chuck reached into the clamshell and removed the crown. It was even more beautiful than they had imagined. It was an elegant ring of golden coral that looked thousands of years old. Clusters of seashells decorated the bottom, and a sparkling gem was at the top of each of its eleven peaks. It didn't shine or sparkle in the light. Rather, golden rays flashed from it, as though the crown itself were made of light.

"I want that crown!" the Kingfish blubbered. "It's mine!" He rushed for Chuck and Dakota, chasing them around the top of the temple. Dakota put the hornpipe up to his lips, but he tripped and dropped the hornpipe before he could play a single note. It clattered down the side of the temple and *BLOOP!* It disappeared in the water.

Chuck and Dakota tossed the crown back and forth, keeping it away from the Kingfish. They were so busy avoiding him that they did not notice Nwar flying up behind them. The black parrot snatched the crown in midair.

Chuck and Dakota froze in terror as Nwar brought the crown to the Kingfish. As he slowly lowered it onto his slimy head, his body tripled in size. He loomed over them, roaring with laughter that shook them to their very core. The crown billowed black smoke that curled around his evil face.

"You little fools!" the Kingfish bellowed in

a deep voice that shook the heavens. "I already told you! It's my ocean! I'm the Boss! I'm the KING!"

Dakota had never seen a fiercer beast in his life. But he suddenly remembered that there was one creature more feared, more terrifying, and more legendary than this giant catfish: HU'MANS.

"No, you're just a bully!" Dakota stood up tall. "And even the meanest bully has something he's afraid of!" With that, Dakota pulled off his cow mask, showing his true face to the monstrous catfish.

The Kingfish's thunderous voice withered to a frightened squeal. "A hu'man? A hu'man?! It's not possible!"

Dakota crept toward the Kingfish, smacking his lips. "That's right, I'm a hu'man! And I'm hungry for a big…baked…catfish!"

Backing up in fear, the hefty Kingfish began to slip and slide on the temple's smooth, flat top. His huge new size was difficult to balance on top of the temple. He stumbled and tumbled, falling down, down, down... right into the mouth of the spider crab. The giant crab happily swallowed the king-sized Kingfish, crown and all.

The stunned pirates looked up at Dakota, standing at the top of the temple.

"Is that a hu'man?" they shrieked. "Run! He'll boil us! He'll fry us! He'll eat us with butter!" Shellfish scattered into the water, swimming away in every direction without looking back. The spider crab let out a monstrous BUUUURRRRRRRPPP! Then he disappeared below the waves, and all was quiet.

Marco flapped up to the top of the temple.

Dakota hadn't put his mask back on yet. He hoped Marco and Ribeye would not see him as a monster.

"I guess-a the Kingfish got too big for his own good," Marco said. He quoted the last line of the poem, "'*Those who bring ruin will earn it as well.*' That pirate brought this on himself."

Marco looked at Dakota's worried hu'man face. He picked up Dakota's cow mask and handed it back to him. "As I said before, little one…I have seen many horrific monsters. But you are not one of them."

"Please don't tell," Dakota whispered. "I don't want to be kicked off the island yet."

Marco smiled, "Don't worry, little one. This is a story no one would believe!"

They all gazed down at the spot where the spider crab had disappeared. "The crown is gone," Marco moaned. "After all this time, all this way…I would very much liked to have just held it."

"No one was supposed to have it," Chuck said.

"I suppose," Marco sighed. "It was the spider crab's job to guard the crown. Now he gets to do that forever." He closed the clamshell's lid. "Come, little ones. If we set sail now, we can be back in Bermooda by sundown."

Chuck and Dakota shared a puzzled look. "Really? All that way by sundown?"

"*Certamente!*" Marco smiled. "We'll just go in a *straight* line."

12
SOME TREASURE HUNT

"So…you fought a whole army of shellfish by yourself?"

The four weary travelers were back home on Bermooda. It had been a whole week since they returned from their voyage. Marco was in his regular spot at the Leaky Tiki. As promised, Chuck had returned Dakota's bandana to its rightful place on the tiki's head.

"Not just a crew," Marco said, waving his wings in the air. "A brigade! An army! A legion of savage shellfish, armed to the gills and led by their pirate king—an enormous, ferocious catfish as tall as the ceiling!"

Chuck and Dakota listened from a nearby table. They didn't join the crowd. After all, they'd already had front-row seats to this story. The plucky chicken's audience continued to grill him with questions.

"So where is this 'Coral Crown'? Do you have it?" asked a tall reddish cow at the front of the crowd.

"Haven't you been listening?" Marco demanded. "It disappeared with the mammoth spider crab, of course!"

"Oh, of course," chuckled a plump cow in a straw hat. "The one as big as your ship."

"Even bigger than my ship!" Marco said.

"Uh-huh. So is this before or after you met the…" the plump cow paused and snickered, "…queen of the fish cows?"

"Sea cows," Marco corrected him. "And it

was after, at Spidercrab Rock!"

"Oh, that's right. The invisible island," another cow said with a guffaw.

"Okay, what about that magic flute you were talking about?" came a voice from the back of the crowd. "Come on, Marco…play us a magic tune!" The whole circle of cows burst into laughter.

"You don't believe me?" Marco clucked angrily, ruffling his feathers. "It is all true! Tell them, Ribeye!"

The surly Ribeye said nothing, but simply addressed the room with his one good eye and nodded his head in agreement with Marco. No one wanted to argue with Ribeye, but no one really seemed to believe Marco, either. They all went back to their tables, mumbling and rolling their eyes.

"Wait! Come back!" Marco pleaded. "*Amici*

Miei! My friends! I'm just getting to the good part!" But it was no use. Story time was over.

With his feathers ruffled, Marco stormed out of the Tiki and back to the *Swashclucker*. Chuck and Dakota followed not too far behind. They found Marco sulking in his cabin, holding the old spyglass.

"It's okay, Marco," Chuck put a hoof on Marco's shoulder. "We know you're telling the truth this time."

Marco picked his head up. "What do you mean, 'this time'?"

"Marco, we looked all over the ship," Dakota said. "We never found any treasures or anything. But it's nice to know at least one of your stories is true."

"One?" Marco laughed. "Try hundreds!" He fluttered across the cabin to the sword collection on his wall and pulled on the handle of the last sword. As he did, the boards on the floor began to move downward, creating a set of steps that led into a hidden room underneath the cabin.

"A secret room?" Chuck gasped.

"Of-a course!" Marco said. "Did you really think-a Marco Pollo would keep his riches where anyone can find them?"

Chuck and Dakota clomped down the steps into a small gallery filled to the brim with treasures. There were ancient artifacts

and mystical objects…glittering jewels and gold coins…there was even a sea snake's head mounted on the wall. It was everything Chuck had hoped for.

Standing in the middle of a room full of riches, they now both knew that they never had to doubt Marco again. And the two of them couldn't help but agree on one thing: that really was some treasure hunt.

LITWI   FLT
Litwin, Mike,
Crown of the Cowibbean /

04/15